NICK JR.

DORA the EXPLORER

Just Like Dora!

by Alison Inches
illustrated by Dave Aikins

Ready-to-Read

Simon Spotlight/Nick Jr.

New York   London   Toronto   Sydney

Based on the TV series *Dora the Explorer*® as seen on Nick Jr.®

SIMON SPOTLIGHT
An imprint of Simon & Schuster Children's Publishing Division
1230 Avenue of the Americas,
New York, New York 10020
Copyright © 2005 Viacom International Inc.
All rights reserved. NICK JR., *Dora the Explorer,*
and all related titles, logos, and characters are trademarks of Viacom International Inc.
All rights reserved, including the right of reproduction in whole or in part in any form.
SIMON SPOTLIGHT, READY-TO-READ, and colophon
are registered trademarks of Simon & Schuster, Inc.
Manufactured in the United States of America

Library of Congress Cataloging-in-Publication Data
Inches, Alison.
Just Like Dora! / by Alison Inches.—1st ed.
p. cm. — (Ready-to-read. Pre-level 1 ; #8)
"Based on the TV series Dora the Explorer as seen on Nick Jr."
Summary: Dora leads her friends on an expedition that ends at an ice cream party.
ISBN 0-689-87675-0
[1. Explorers—Fiction.] I. Dora the explorer (Television program) II. Title. III. Series.
PZ7.I355Fo 2004
[E]—dc22
2004010742

Hi! I am Dora.

Do you like surprises?

Then follow me!

Hop across the rocks!

Hop! Hop! Hop!

Splash in the water!

Just like me!

Row across the lake!

Row! Row! Row!

Slide down the hill!

Just like me!

Are we there yet?

Not yet!

Swing on the vines!

Swing! Swing! Swing!

Jump over the logs!

Just like me!

Here we are!

Guess what we see!

An ice-cream party!

Yummy!

We did it!

Dora's Picnic

by Christine Ricci
illustrated by Susan Hall

Ready-to-Read

Simon Spotlight/Nick Jr.

New York   London   Toronto   Sydney

Based on the TV series *Dora the Explorer*® as seen on Nick Jr.®

SIMON SPOTLIGHT
An imprint of Simon & Schuster Children's Publishing Division
1230 Avenue of the Americas,
New York, New York 10020
Copyright © 2003 Viacom International Inc.
All rights reserved. NICKELODEON, NICK JR., *Dora the Explorer,*
and all related titles, logos, and characters are trademarks of Viacom International Inc.
All rights reserved, including the right of reproduction in whole or in part in any form.
READY-TO-READ, SIMON SPOTLIGHT, and colophon
are registered trademarks of Simon & Schuster.
Manufactured in the United States of America

Ricci, Christine.
Dora's picnic / by Christine Ricci.
p. cm.—(Ready-to-read. Level 1, Dora the explorer ; 1)
Summary: Dora and her animal friends all contribute something to bring to
a picnic at Play Park. Features rebuses.
ISBN 0-689-85238-X
1. Rebuses. [1. Picnicking—Fiction. 2. Animals—Fiction. 3. Parks—Fiction. 4. Rebuses.]
I. Title. II. Series.
PZ7.R355 Do 2003
[E]—dc21
2002004518

Hi! I am . We are
going to a picnic at Play
Park! Play Park has a ,
SLIDE

a , and .
SANDBOX   SWINGS

My **mami** is helping me make  -and-

PEANUT-BUTTER   JELLY

sandwiches for the picnic.

 is my best friend.

BOOTS

He loves 🍌!

BANANAS

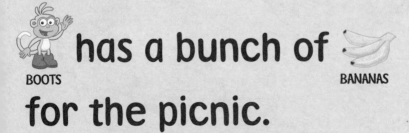

BOOTS has a bunch of BANANAS for the picnic.

BENNY is riding his BICYCLE to the picnic.

He is carrying  juice
APPLE
in his 🧺.
BASKET

Here comes the .

BIG RED CHICKEN

The  has a big  of

BIG RED CHICKEN   BAG

 for the picnic.

POPCORN

Yummy!

Look!  **BABY BLUE BIRD** has a bowl of fruit in her  **WAGON**.

The fruit bowl has ,
BANANAS

, and .
APPLES   GRAPES

What did 🐿 bring to the picnic?

TICO

TICO brought .
BREAD

The is filled with
BREAD

and !
BLUEBERRIES   NUTS

ISA made **CUPCAKES** to share with everyone.

I like chocolate **CUPCAKES**
with **PINK** icing. What kind
do you like?

Look out for 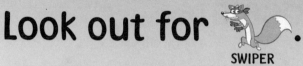 SWIPER.
He will try to swipe
the food we brought.

is hiding behind
SWIPER

the 🌳.
TREE

Say, "Swiper, no swiping!"

Yay! You stopped !
SWIPER

We made it to Play Park!

This 🏁 is perfect for

TABLE

our picnic. But first we

want to play!

TICO likes to go down the **SLIDE**.

is making a

BABY BLUE BIRD SAND CASTLE

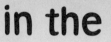 .

SANDBOX

The  pushes
BIG RED CHICKEN   BOOTS

and  on the .
ISA   SWINGS

This is the best picnic!
We can all share the food.
What would **you** bring
to a picnic?

Follow Those Feet!

by Christine Ricci
illustrated by Susan Hall

Ready-to-Read

Simon Spotlight/Nick Jr.

New York   London   Toronto   Sydney

Based on the TV series *Dora the Explorer*® as seen on Nick Jr.®

SIMON SPOTLIGHT
An imprint of Simon & Schuster Children's Publishing Division
1230 Avenue of the Americas,
New York, New York 10020
Copyright © 2003 Viacom International Inc.
All rights reserved. NICKELODEON, NICK JR., *Dora the Explorer,*
and all related titles, logos, and characters are trademarks of Viacom International Inc.
All rights reserved, including the right of reproduction in whole or in part in any form.
READY-TO-READ, SIMON SPOTLIGHT, and colophon are
registered trademarks of Simon & Schuster.
Manufactured in the United States of America

Library of Congress Cataloging-in-Publication Data
Ricci, Christine.
Follow Those Feet! / by Christine Ricci.
p. cm.—(Ready-to-read ; 2)
Summary: Dora and Boots have found some strange footprints in the sandbox,
and need the reader's help to discover who—or what—made them.
Features rebuses.
ISBN 0-689-85239-8
1. Rebuses. [1. Animal tracks—Fiction. 2. Footprints—Fiction. 3. Rebuses.]
I. Title. II. Series.
PZ7.R355 Wh 2003
[E]—dc21
2002004826

Hi! I am  **DORA**. **BOOTS** and I found some **FOOTPRINTS** in the **SANDBOX**.
I wonder who made them.

Do you know?

Did I make these ?

FOOTPRINTS

No, my feet are small.

I did not make these .

FOOTPRINTS

Did  make these ?
BOOTS   FOOTPRINTS
No, his   are shaped
       FOOTPRINTS
like an oval. He did not
make these   .
              FOOTPRINTS

Who made
these 🐾 ?
FOOTPRINTS

We can follow them to
find out.

Hello,  !
BIG RED CHICKEN

Did you make these ?
FOOTPRINTS

No, his feet have three toes! He did not make these .

FOOTPRINTS

Did the  make these ?

HORSE

FOOTPRINTS

No, the horse wears  **HORSESHOES** on her feet. She did not make these **FOOTPRINTS**.

Did the 🐰 make the 🐾?

RABBIT   FOOTPRINTS

No, she has two long feet

and two short feet.

She did not make these

FOOTPRINTS

Did the  make these
SNAKE
? No, the does
FOOTPRINTS   SNAKE
not have feet!

He slides across the ground. He did not make these .

FOOTPRINTS

Do you see ? Did make these 👣 ?

No,  **SWIPER** is sneaky!

He tiptoes. He did not

make these **FOOTPRINTS**.

The go all the way to
FOOTPRINTS
the beach!

They go by the 🐚🐚
SHELLS

toward the 🏰 .
SAND CASTLE

Now do you know who
made these ?
FOOTPRINTS

It was 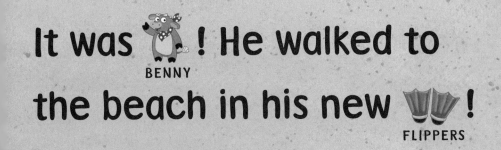 ! He walked to
the beach in his new !

Yay! We did it! We found out who made the 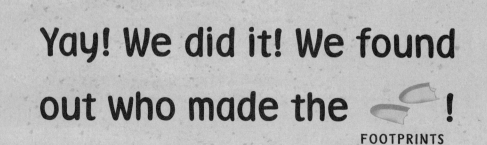 !

FOOTPRINTS

Dora in the Deep Sea

by Christine Ricci
illustrated by Robert Roper

Ready-to-Read

Simon Spotlight/Nick Jr.

New York   London   Toronto   Sydney

Based on the TV series *Dora the Explorer*® as seen on Nick Jr.®

SIMON SPOTLIGHT
An imprint of Simon & Schuster Children's Publishing Division
1230 Avenue of the Americas, New York, New York 10020
Copyright © 2003 Viacom International Inc.
All rights reserved. NICKELODEON, NICK JR., *Dora the Explorer,* and all related titles,
logos, and characters are trademarks of Viacom International Inc.
All rights reserved, including the right of reproduction
in whole or in part in any form.
READY-TO-READ, SIMON SPOTLIGHT, and colophon are
registered trademarks of Simon & Schuster.
Manufactured in the United States of America

Library of Congress Cataloging-in-Publication Data
Ricci, Christine.
Dora in the deep sea / by Christine Ricci ; illustrated by Robert Roper.— 1st ed.
p. cm. — (Dora the explorer ready-to-read ; #3)
"Based on the TV series Dora the Explorer(tm) as seen on Nick Jr."
Summary: Dora and Boots go down deep into the sea in a submarine to help Pirate
Pig find his lost treasure chest. Features rebuses.
ISBN 0-689-85845-0 (pbk.)
1. Rebuses. [1. Buried treasure—Fiction. 2. Marine animals—Fiction. 3. Rebuses.]
I. Roper, Robert, ill. II. Dora the explorer (Television program) III. Title. IV. Series:
Ready-to-read. Level 1, Dora the explorer ; #3.
PZ7.R355 Dl 2003
[E]—dc22
2003010523

Hi! I am  **DORA**. This is **BOOTS**.
And here is our friend,
PIRATE PIG. **PIRATE PIG** looks sad.
What is wrong, **PIRATE PIG**?

"I have lost my  !"

TREASURE CHEST

says  . "The

PIRATE PIG   **TREASURE CHEST**

fell off my  and

SHIP

into the  !"

SEA

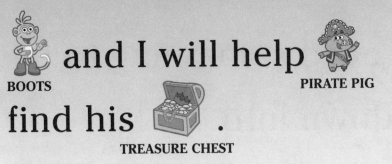 and I will help  find his  .

BOOTS

PIRATE PIG

TREASURE CHEST

Will you help too?

We need something to take
us down into the  .
SEA
What can take us into the
SEA ?

A  can take us down

SUBMARINE

into the  !

SEA

Ooh, we are going down

into the  .

SEA

Look! A  !

SAND CASTLE

Hello, !

KING CRAB

There is a  with
FISH   SPOTS

by the .
ROCK

I see a  . . . and a funny

STARFISH

clownfish!

Boots spots a  🐢.
GREEN TURTLE

Pirate Pig sees 🟡 .
YELLOW SEA HORSES

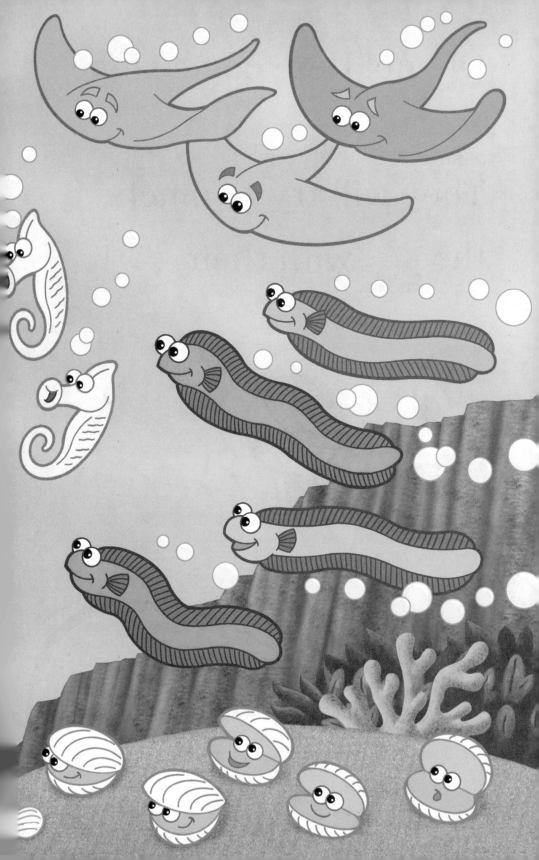

Oh, no! Here come some

!

LOBSTERS

They will try to pinch

the  with their !

SUBMARINE   **CLAWS**

We drove the  **SUBMARINE**

past the ![lobsters]! **LOBSTERS**

Now we need to find

the ![treasure chest] . **TREASURE CHEST**

Hooray! We found the  !

TREASURE CHEST

But we have to watch out

for 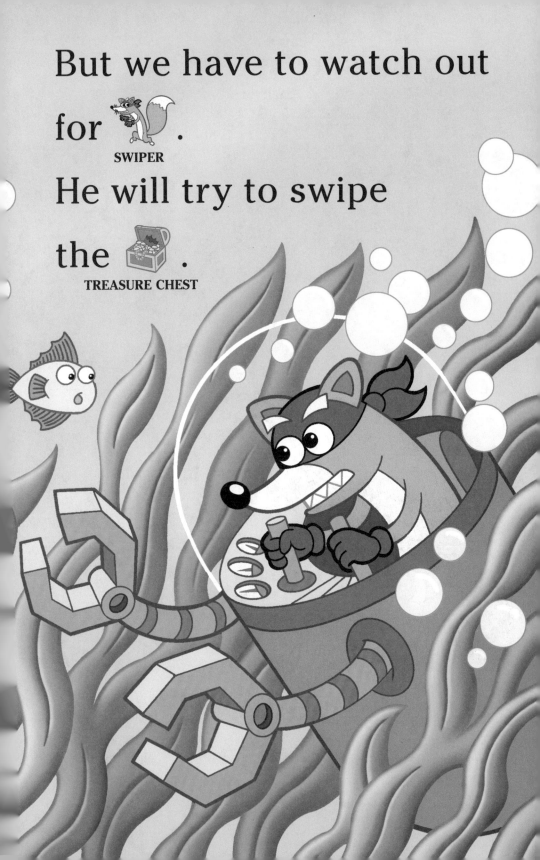.

SWIPER

He will try to swipe

the 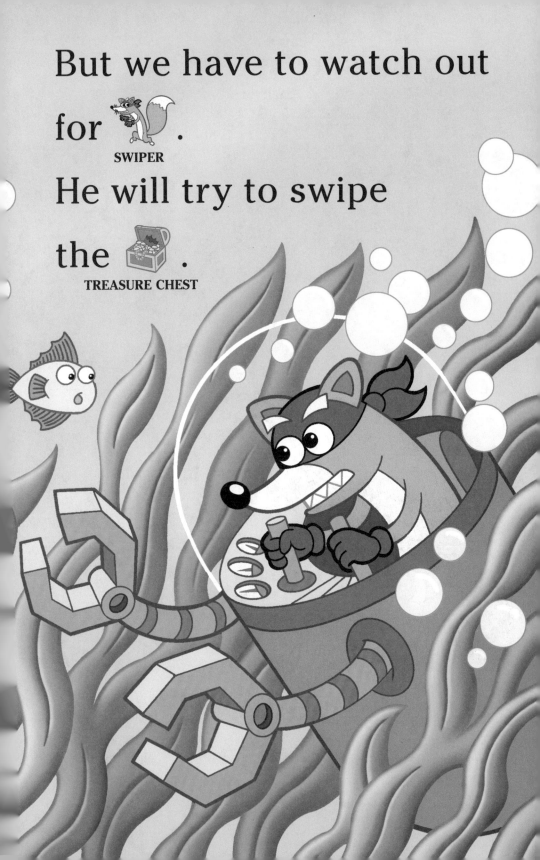.

TREASURE CHEST

Do you see  ?
SWIPER

Look!  **SWIPER** is behind the 🐋 ! **WHALE**

He is going to swipe

the 🧰 ! **TREASURE CHEST**

We have to say " , no swiping!"

SWIPER

You helped us stop SWIPER!

Yay!  has his ▣ !

PIRATE PIG   TREASURE CHEST

Thank you for helping!

I Love My Papi!

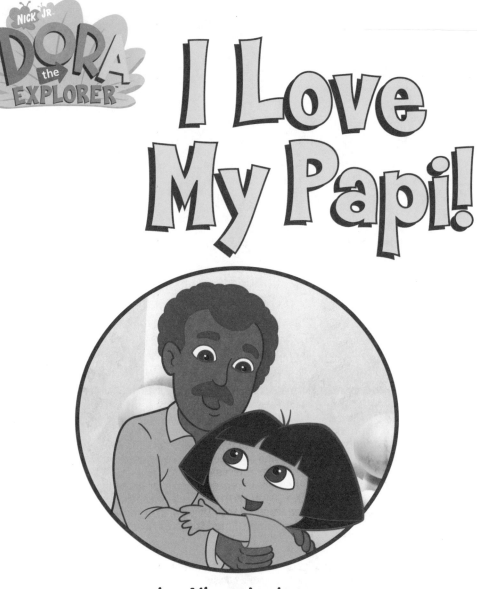

by Alison Inches
illustrated by Dave Aikins

Ready-to-Read

Simon Spotlight/Nick Jr.

New York   London   Toronto   Sydney

Based on the TV series *Dora the Explorer*® as seen on Nick Jr.®

SIMON SPOTLIGHT
An imprint of Simon & Schuster Children's Publishing Division
1230 Avenue of the Americas
New York, New York 10020
Copyright © 2004 Viacom International Inc.

All rights reserved. NICKELODEON, NICK JR., *Dora the Explorer,*
and all related titles, logos, and characters are registered trademarks of
Viacom International Inc.
All rights reserved, including the right of reproduction in whole or in part in any form.
READY-TO-READ, SIMON SPOTLIGHT, and colophon are
registered trademarks of Simon & Schuster.

Manufactured in the United States of America

Library of Congress Cataloging-in-Publication Data
Inches, Alison.
I love my Papi! / by Alison Inches ; illustrated by Dave Aikens.—1st ed.
p. cm. — (Ready-to-read)
"Based on the TV series Dora the Explorer as seen on Nick Jr."
Summary: Dora and her Papi play baseball, go to the beach, read books, and do lots of
other fun things together.
ISBN 0-689-86495-7
[1. Fathers and daughters—Fiction.] I. Saunders, Zina, ill. II. Dora the explorer
(Television program) III. Title. IV. Series.
PZ7.I355 Iae 2004
[E]—dc22
2003014360

My and I love to do things together!

PAPI

 taught me a super soccer kick. Look, I kicked the ⚽ into the 🥅 !

PAPI

SOCCER BALL

GOAL

We also love playing .

BASEBALL

 coaches my team.

PAPI

He taught us how to swing the  BAT and slide into home BASE.

On weekends  and I
PAPI
ride 🚲 together.
BIKES

Or sail on a .
BOAT

Sometimes we go to the together.

BEACH

We build giant  and
SAND CASTLES

play in the 🌊.
WAVES

My  is a really good ▮.
PAPI   COOK

He taught me how to bake

a special 🎂 and make
CAKE

yummy 🥪.
SANDWICHES

Sometimes we pack a PICNIC

and share it with my

friend BOOTS.

My 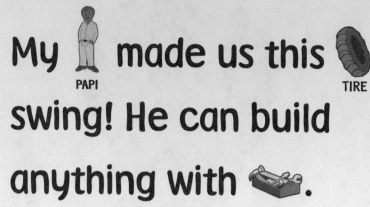 made us this TIRE swing! He can build anything with TOOLS.

PAPI

One time  took us to the . loved the .

CIRCUS

PAPI

BOOTS

CLOWNS

Then  bought us and

PAPI

POPCORN

for a treat.

STRAWBERRY **ICE CREAM**

Yum! Yum!

At the end of every day tucks me into .

PAPI

BED

Then we read a .
BOOK
I like BOOKS about ANIMALS.

 says, "I love my !"
PAPI   DORA

And I say, "I love my !"
                                    PAPI

Say "Cheese!"

by Christine Ricci
illustrated by Steven Savitsky

Ready-to-Read

Simon Spotlight/Nick Jr.

New York   London   Toronto   Sydney

Based on the TV series *Dora the Explorer*® as seen on Nick Jr.®

SIMON SPOTLIGHT
An imprint of Simon & Schuster Children's Publishing Division
1230 Avenue of the Americas
New York, New York 10020
Copyright © 2004 Viacom International Inc.
All rights reserved. NICKELODEON, NICK JR., *Dora the Explorer,*
and all related titles, logos, and characters are registered trademarks
of Viacom International Inc.
All rights reserved, including the right of reproduction in whole or in part in any form.
READY-TO-READ, SIMON SPOTLIGHT, and colophon are
registered trademarks of Simon & Schuster.
Manufactured in the United States of America

Library of Congress Cataloging-in-Publication Data
Ricci, Christine.
Say cheese! / by Christine Ricci ; illustrated by Steven Savitsky.— 1st ed.
p. cm. — (Ready-to-read. Level 1, Dora the explorer ; 5)
Summary: To cheer up Boots the monkey who is sick, Dora and her animal friends make
him a photograph album. Features rebuses.
ISBN 0-689-86496-5 (pbk.)
1. Rebuses. [1. Photography—Fiction. 2. Animals—Fiction. 3. Rebuses.] I. Title. II. Series.
PZ7.R355Say 2004
[E]—dc21
2003007583

Hi! I am DORA . My friend BOOTS is sick today.

How can we cheer him up?

I know! We can visit

BOOTS

at his  .

TREE HOUSE

And we can use my

CAMERA

to take pictures of things

 likes.

BOOTS

 would love a picture

BOOTS

of  and .

BACKPACK   MAP

Say "  !"

CHEESE

We are at  Mountain.
STAR

Mountain is filled
STAR

with .
STARS

loves to play with
BOOTS

the !
STARS

Look! There is  .

TOOL STAR

 has all kinds of  .

TOOL STAR   TOOLS

Say "  !"

CHEESE

Here is a fruit garden.

Which fruit does  like?

Yes, BOOTS loves BANANAS!

Who else loves ?
BANANAS

The 🦉!
BIRD

Say "🧀!"
CHEESE

likes silly things too!

BOOTS

The are making silly

CROCODILES

faces.

Ha, ha, ha! Smile,  !

CROCODILES

Say "  !"

CHEESE

Do you see more

silly things?

 has baked a  CAKE

for  BOOTS .

Yummy!

 made a  for .

BENNY CARD BOOTS

 and  look at

ISA BENNY

the .

CAMERA

Say "!"

CHEESE

Here is an  cart.

ICE-CREAM

loves !

BOOTS   ICE CREAM

Say " !"

CHEESE

Uh-oh. Do you see

someone behind the

🍦 cart?

ICE-CREAM

It is  !

SWIPER

 wants to swipe

SWIPER

our  .

CAMERA

We have to stop .

Say " , no swiping!"

Yay! We stopped !

Hey, there is !

TICO will give us a ride
to the TREE HOUSE in his CAR.
Say "CHEESE!"

Hooray! We made it to the

TREE HOUSE.

And **BOOTS** loves all the

pictures!

We cheered up .

BOOTS

Thanks for helping!

Oh, I have to take  ^{ONE}

more picture.

 wants a picture of

BOOTS

you!

Say "  !"

CHEESE

Eggs for Everyone!

by Laura Driscoll
illustrated by A&J Studios

Ready-to-Read

Simon Spotlight/Nick Jr.

New York   London   Toronto   Sydney

Based on the TV series *Dora the Explorer*® as seen on Nick Jr.®

SIMON SPOTLIGHT
An imprint of Simon & Schuster Children's Publishing Division
1230 Avenue of the Americas
New York, New York 10020
Copyright © 2005 Viacom International Inc. All rights reserved.
NICKELODEON, NICK JR., *Dora the Explorer,* and all related titles, logos, and characters
are registered trademarks of Viacom International Inc.
All rights reserved, including the right of reproduction in whole or in part in any form.
READY-TO-READ, SIMON SPOTLIGHT, and colophon are
registered trademarks of Simon & Schuster, Inc.
Manufactured in the United States of America

Library of Congress Cataloging-in-Publication Data
Driscoll, Laura.
Eggs for everyone! / by Laura Driscoll ; illustrated by A&J Studios.— 1st ed.
p. cm. — (Dora the explorer ready-to-read ; #7)
"Based on the TV series Dora the Explorer as seen on Nick Jr."—T.p.
Summary: Dora and her friend Boots decorate eggs for their families and friends.
ISBN 0-689-87176-7
[1. Egg decoration—Fiction.] I. A&J Studios. II. Title.
III. Ready-to-read. Level 1, Dora the explorer ; #7.
PZ7.D79Eg 2005
[E]—dc22
2004004969

Hi! I am .

DORA

and I are coloring

BOOTS

for our friends.

EGGS

We are making  BLUE EGGS

and YELLOW EGGS and

PINK EGGS and ORANGE EGGS .

We put stickers

on some .
EGGS

We have stickers of FLOWERS

and  TEDDY BEARS and  STARS

and other things too.

Now we can take the 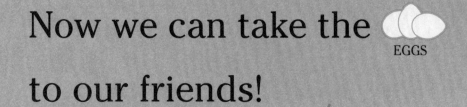 to our friends!

There is .
ISA

loves .
ISA   FLOWERS

Do you know which
EGG

we made for ?
ISA

Look! It is 's
BOOTS

mommy and daddy.

They live with
BOOTS

in a .
TREE HOUSE

Which  did make for them?

EGG   BOOTS

 likes to drive

his little YELLOW CAR .

Which EGG

did we make for TICO ?

DIEGO loves **BABY JAGUAR**.

Which **EGG** did we make

for **DIEGO**?

I love my 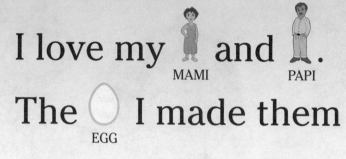 and 👤.
MAMI   PAPI

The 🥚 I made them
EGG

shows how much.

Which  is for MAMI and PAPI?

 loves 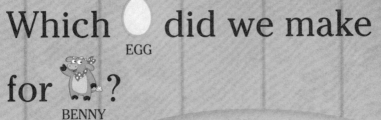.

BENNY   TEDDY BEARS

Which ⬭ did we make

EGG

for 🐄?

BENNY

 is a

ABUELA

⭐ catcher

STAR

just like me.

Which ⬭ EGG is for 👤 ABUELA ?

Oh, look!

There is one  left
EGG

in the BASKET.

Who is it for?

Need a hint? 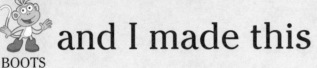 and I made this for someone who helped us today.

BOOTS

EGG

BOOTS and I made this  **EGG**

for you!

We hope you like it!

The Halloween Cat

by Christine Ricci
illustrated by Zina Saunders

Ready-to-Read

Simon Spotlight/Nick Jr.

New York   London   Toronto   Sydney

Based on the TV series *Dora the Explorer*® as seen on Nick Jr.®

SIMON SPOTLIGHT
An imprint of Simon & Schuster Children's Publishing Division
1230 Avenue of the Americas
New York, New York 10020
Copyright © 2004 Viacom International Inc. All rights reserved.
NICKELODEON, NICK JR., *Dora the Explorer,* and all related titles, logos, and characters
are registered trademarks of Viacom International Inc.
All rights reserved, including the right of reproduction in whole or in part in any form.
READY-TO-READ, SIMON SPOTLIGHT, and colophon are
registered trademarks of Simon & Schuster, Inc.
Manufactured in the United States of America

Library of Congress Cataloging-in-Publication Data
Ricci, Christine.
The Halloween cat / by Christine Ricci ; [illustrated by] Zina Saunders.—1st ed.
p. cm. —(Ready-to-read)
"Based on the TV series Dora the Explorer as seen on Nick Jr"—T.p. verso.
Summary: Dora and Boots help a small black cat find its way home to the Candy Castle on
Halloween. Features rebuses.
ISBN 0-689-86799-9 (pbk.)
1. Rebuses. [1. Halloween—Fiction. 2. Cats—Fiction. 3. Rebuses.] I. Saunders, Zina, ill.
II. Dora the explorer (Television program) III. Title. IV. Ready-to-read. Level 1,
Dora the explorer.
PZ7.R355 Hal 2004
[E]—dc22
2003018335

Hi, I am 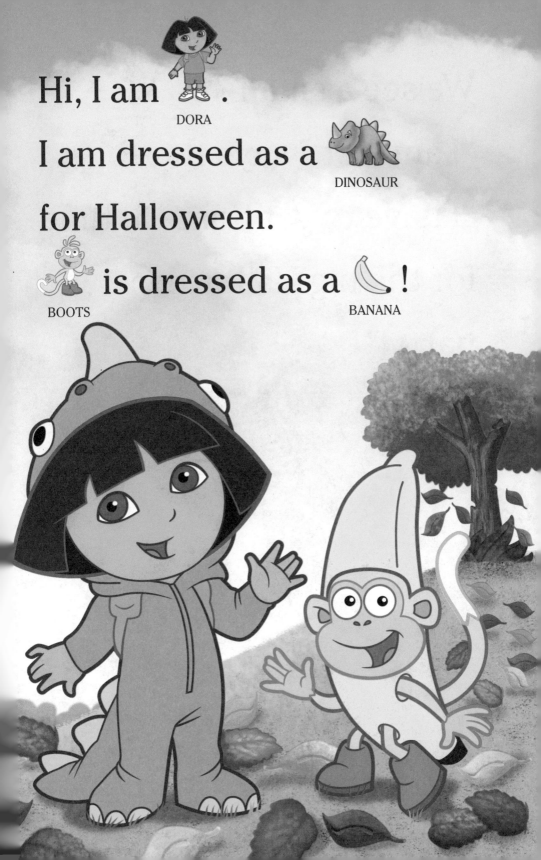 .
DORA

I am dressed as a DINOSAUR

for Halloween.

BOOTS is dressed as a BANANA !

We see a small 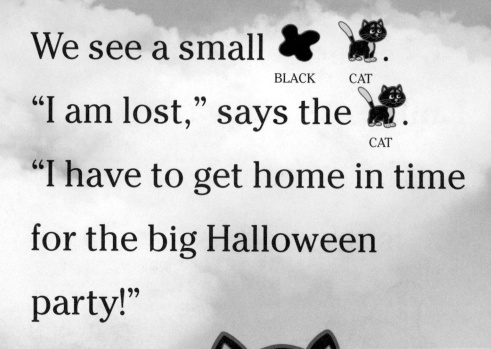.

BLACK   CAT

"I am lost," says the 🐈.

CAT

"I have to get home in time

for the big Halloween

party!"

and I will help

the .

Will you help

too?

The  knows where
the MAP  lives.
CAT
"The  lives in the
CAT
 with the ,"
CANDY CASTLE   GOOD WITCH
says .
MAP

We have to go to the
HAUNTED HOUSE

and into the  to get to
SPOOKY FOREST

the .
CANDY CASTLE

We are at the .

HAUNTED HOUSE

It is dark inside!

We need something to

help us see in the dark.

Can you spot the 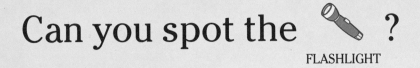 ?

FLASHLIGHT

There are many  DOORS

in the HAUNTED HOUSE.

A  says, "Find the

GHOST

with 7 ."

SEVEN   SPIDERS

DOOR

Yay! We made it out of the .

HAUNTED HOUSE

Now we will go to the  .

SPOOKY FOREST

Do you see the  ?

SPOOKY FOREST

Uh-oh, here is a  .

GATE

says an

MAP ORANGE KEY

will open the .

GATE

Do you see an  ?
ORANGE KEY

Watch out!

will try to swipe the .
SWIPER   KEY

Say " , no swiping!"
SWIPER

Yay! We stopped 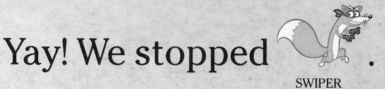 .

And we opened the !

SWIPER

GATE

says the RED LEAVES

MAP   RED   LEAVES

will lead us out of the

.

SPOOKY FOREST

We made it out of the 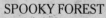 !

SPOOKY FOREST

Now we have to find .

CANDY CASTLE

Here we are at  .
CANDY CASTLE

But how do we get in?

"Use the  !" says
BROOMSTICK

the  .
CAT

Wow! We are flying!

Hello,  !

GOOD WITCH

We did it! The  is home

CAT

with the .

GOOD WITCH

Happy Halloween!